ENGELBERT
Moves the House

Written by Tom Paxton   Illustrated by Don Vanderbeek

ScottForesman
A Division of HarperCollins

W9-CCM-170

In a teeny, tiny house
lives the quiet Mrs. Mouse.

2

It's so noisy every day
that she wants to move away.

3

Mrs. Lion shouts, "Hello!"
Hippo giggles, "Ho, ho, ho!"

Monkeys chatter from tree to tree.
Oh, how noisy they can be!

5

Engelbert walks down the street
in the steamy summer heat.

He can see the quiet mouse
looking sad inside her house.

"I can help you move your house,"
Engelbert tells Mrs. Mouse.

8

He gives the house a great, big tug
and holds it with a great, big hug.

9

Engelbert finds a quiet, little town.
Here he puts the teeny house down.

Mrs. Mouse makes him lunch
and a pot of jungle punch.

Engelbert plays a little song,
and all the mice sing along.

12

13

Mrs. Mouse is safe inside.

Engelbert's smile is very wide.

He shouts, "May you be happy here!"
And all the mice begin to cheer.
HURRAY FOR ENGELBERT!

16